Magic Kitten

Firelight Friends

To Sophie, a nervous neighborly kitty.

GROSSET & DUNLAP
Published by the Penguin Group
Penguin Group (USA) LLC, 375 Hudson Street, New York, New York 10014, USA

USA | Canada | UK | Ireland | Australia | New Zealand | India | South Africa | China

penguin.com
A Penguin Random House Company

Text copyright © 2007 by Sue Bentley. Illustrations copyright © 2007 by Angela Swan. Cover illustration copyright © 2007 by Andrew Farley. All rights reserved. First printed in Great Britain in 2007 by Penguin Books Ltd. First published in the United States in 2014 by Grosset & Dunlap, a division of Penguin Young Readers Group, 345 Hudson Street, New York, New York 10014. GROSSET & DUNLAP is a trademark of Penguin Group (USA) LLC. Printed in the USA.

Library of Congress Cataloging-in-Publication Data is available.

ISBN 978-0-448-46788-7   10 9 8 7 6 5 4 3 2 1

Firelight Friends

SUE BENTLEY

Illustrated by Angela Swan

Grosset & Dunlap
An Imprint of Penguin Group (USA) LLC

★ Prologue ★

"Uncle Ebony!" gasped the young white lion as an enormous adult lion appeared on a nearby ridge. There was a flash of dazzling white light, and sparkles sprinkled the ground where the young white lion had stood. There now crouched a tiny kitten with fluffy white fur and four black-tipped paws.

Flame's tiny kitten body trembled as he edged slowly backward toward a grove of thorn trees. He could hear Ebony's angry roar and imagined his fierce, ice-cold eyes.

Suddenly a huge paw, almost as big as Flame's entire body, reached out from the deep shade and scooped him up. Flame gave a whine of terror and laid his ears back. This was it. One of his uncle's spies had found him!

But instead of being grabbed by the scruff of his neck and dragged out into the open, he found himself being swept further back into the safety of the trees. An old gray lion looked down at him.

"Cirrus! Thank you, old friend," Flame mewed gratefully.

Cirrus bowed his head respectfully. "I

am glad to see you again, Prince Flame. But it is still not safe for you to stay. Ebony is determined to take the Lion Throne from you. He will never stop searching for you."

Flame's bright emerald eyes sparked with anger. "This kingdom is mine by right! Perhaps I should face my uncle for it now!"

The old lion's worn teeth showed in a smile. "Bravely said, but Ebony is still too strong for you. Use this disguise and go back to the other world to hide."

Flame nodded. "I will, but only until my powers are stronger. Then I will return to overthrow Ebony and his rule will end!"

"May that be soon, my prince," Cirrus rumbled with pride and affection.

Above them both, on the high ridge, Ebony slowly turned his enormous head, and his mouth opened in a terrifying roar. He leaped down and began charging toward the thorn trees, his mighty paws eating up the dusty ground.

"He knows you're here! Go now. Save yourself," Cirrus urged.

Sparks ignited in Flame's white fur as he felt the power building inside him. His four black-tipped paws flexed, and he gave a tiny mew as he felt himself falling. Falling . . .

Chapter
ONE

"I can't believe I'm finally here. I've been looking forward to summer camp for so long!" Kara Parkes said excitedly, as she hugged her mom and dad good-bye.

"Now, you have a great time and make lots of new friends," Mrs. Parkes said, smiling. "And try not to worry about Amber."

Amber was Kara's pony. Kara had
been riding her when a fox had run across
the pony's path, and she had reared up in
fright. Although Kara had been thrown,
she wasn't hurt, but Amber had strained
her leg.

"Okay, Mom," Kara said, feeling
an unwelcome stab of guilt for leaving
Amber by herself.

Her dad seemed to know what she

was thinking. "We'll make sure that Amber gets lots of extra love. You just concentrate on enjoying yourself," Mr. Parkes said, ruffling his daughter's sandy, shoulder-length hair.

Kara smiled at him. "Thanks, Dad. Will you give her a hug from me every single day? And let me know what the vet says when he checks on her leg?"

"Sure thing!" her dad promised.

Kara waved as her parents got into their car and drove off down the steep, winding road. "Bye! See you in two weeks," she called.

Clouds passing overhead made shadows on the green slopes of the nearby mountains. When Kara couldn't see the car anymore, she turned and went toward Torc House, where a big sign over the door read TH ADVENTURE VACATIONS. As she went inside and wandered upstairs toward the girls' dormitories, sounds of talking and laughter floated down to her.

Kara went slowly, trying to remember the way from when she had been shown around earlier. She had almost reached the dorms when a girl came dashing toward her. She was small and slim, with silky blond hair and a pretty face. "Are you in Starlings?" she asked.

Kara nodded, remembering how excited she had been at home to tear open the letter from TH Adventure Vacations and find out exactly which dorm she was going to be in.

"Me too. I think we're in here," the girl said, pushing open the nearest door.

"Quick, let's get in! I'm Felicity, by the way."

"Hi . . . er, I'm Kara," Kara said, blinking in surprise as Felicity virtually hauled her into the room. "What's the hurry?"

"Duh! Don't you *want* to get the best beds?" Felicity leaped across the room and jumped straight onto one of two beds near the window. "This is mine. You can have the one next to me!"

Kara looked around the small room with its three identical beds and dressers. The cheerful patterned rug matched the curtains, and there was a comfy chair, with a patchwork cushion, in one corner. Three suitcases were piled on the rug. Kara's suitcase, which her dad had brought upstairs for her, was on the bottom.

Kara spotted a bed by itself against the wall. "I think I'd rather have this one," she decided, going over to sit on it.

"Suit yourself," Felicity murmured, flicking back her long hair. She flounced off her bed and began opening her suitcases.

"I'm glad to see that you're settling in, girls," called a cheerful voice from the doorway.

Kara turned to see a tall woman with curly brown hair, wearing a tomato-red T-shirt with TH ADVENTURE VACATIONS printed on it. It was Miss Cross, the activities organizer.

Miss Cross smiled. "I just found your other roommate looking a little lost. Come in, dear," she said, beckoning to someone behind her. "You'll be sharing with Kara and Felicity."

A somewhat tall, stocky girl stepped into the room and stood looking down at the floor.

"This is Cherry Bradford, girls," Miss Cross announced. "I'm sure you'll all make friends soon. Remember to listen for the bell and come downstairs for lunch. See you all later!"

"Cherry!" Felicity spluttered as soon as

Miss Cross left. "Have you ever heard such a weird name? And how old are you?" she asked suspiciously. "You can't come to this camp if you're more than twelve."

Cherry shuffled her feet and went bright pink. "I'm ten and three quarters. Mom says I'm big for my age."

Kara smiled at Cherry, wishing that Felicity would shut up. "It's a really unusual name. I bet people always remember it," she said.

Cherry shot Kara a grateful look. "My mom had a craving for cherries when she was pregnant. So she called me Cherry when I was born," she said quietly.

"Oh well, it could have been worse. It's lucky she wasn't craving pineapples!" Kara joked.

Cherry's eyes crinkled and she started laughing. Kara joined in. "What's so funny? I don't get it," Felicity said.

"Cherry could have been called Pineapple!" Kara explained, laughing even harder.

Felicity looked blank. "That's stupid! I

think you're lying. I bet you're laughing at me. This is the first time I've been away from home, so you should be extra nice to me instead of picking on me!"

Kara was surprised to see tears in Felicity's blue eyes. She decided to make a big effort to like her, even if Felicity did act more like a spoiled four-year-old. "We weren't picking on you, honest," she said.

"No, we weren't," Cherry agreed. She fished around in her jean-jacket pocket for a bar of chocolate. After breaking it into three pieces, she gave some to Kara and Felicity.

"Thanks," Kara said, nibbling her piece.

Felicity handed her chocolate back to Cherry. "I don't eat candy," she sniffled.

"It's bad for your teeth. Anyway, it's against the rules to keep food in the dorm."

Cherry put Felicity's piece of chocolate into her mouth and held up her empty hands. "Well, I don't *have* any food now, do I?"

Kara bit back a grin.

Felicity glared at them both and then went back to her unpacking. She took a small threadbare teddy bear out of her suitcase and gave it a hug. "Don't either of you dare touch Marvin," she warned, propping the teddy bear against her pillows. "I've had him since I was a baby, and I can't go to sleep without him."

Just then, a bell rang somewhere in the building.

"Lunch!" Felicity jumped off her bed

and shot toward the door. "Come on, you two!"

Cherry paused in the open doorway. "But shouldn't we wait for K—" she began.

"I'll only take a second. I just want to put my sneakers on," Kara said.

"She can follow us. Come on," Felicity urged, dragging Cherry outside.

Kara's heart sank as she wondered how she was going to put up with Felicity's bossiness. She pulled her sneakers out of her suitcase and then sat down on the rug by her bed to take off her sandals.

But then suddenly a flash of bright white light filled the room.

"Oh!" Kara gasped, blinded for a moment.

A crackling sound just like electricity came from the comfy chair across the room. Blinking hard, Kara peered slowly over her bed and saw a tiny, fluffy white kitten with four little black feet sitting on the patchwork cushion. Its soft fur seemed to be glowing faintly with hundreds of tiny sparkles.

Kara frowned, puzzled. She didn't

remember Felicity or Cherry bringing a toy cat with them. "Wow! You look so real! I wonder where you came from?" she said, starting to push herself to her feet.

The tiny kitten blinked up at her with frightened emerald-green eyes. "I come from far away. Can you help me to hide?" it mewed.

Chapter
TWO

Kara's jaw dropped, and she
collapsed back into a heap on the rug.
Had the kitten really just answered
her? She stared at it in complete
astonishment.

"Is this some kind of trick?" she
gasped, whipping around to see if
Felicity was peeping through the door.
She struck Kara as the sort of person

who might put an electrical toy on the chair to get a reaction.

The kitten pricked up its tiny white ears. It was absolutely gorgeous, with soft fuzzy fur and the biggest emerald eyes Kara had ever seen. Its four black feet made it look as if it were wearing tiny cute shoes.

"This is not a trick. I am Prince Flame. Who are you?" the kitten meowed.

"Kara . . . Parkes." Kara gulped, rising to her knees. "I'm . . . at Torc House for summer camp. Did you say *Prince* Flame?" She could still hardly believe that she actually was having a conversation with a kitten.

Flame lifted his tiny chin, and his emerald eyes flashed with pride. "Yes. I am heir to the Lion Throne. But my uncle Ebony has stolen it from me and rules in my place!"

"But . . . but you're such a tiny kitten," Kara said, her curiosity starting to get the better of her shock.

Flame sat up indignantly. "I will show you. Stay back!" he mewed.

Before Kara could say anything, there was another silver flash, so bright that she had to look away again. When Kara looked back, the tiny kitten had vanished and in its place stood a majestic young white lion with glowing emerald eyes.

"Do not be afraid. I will not harm you," Flame said in a deep velvety growl.

Kara took a deep breath and tried very hard to stay calm. "Okay! I . . . I believe you," she stammered.

With a final blinding flash, Flame reappeared as the tiny white kitten with four black feet. "My uncle sends his spies to find me. I must hide now. Will you help me?" he mewed, trembling all over.

Kara was still shocked from seeing Flame as his true lion self, but she realized that right now he was just an adorable, frightened little kitten. She felt her soft heart melting as she leaned forward and picked him up.

As the sparks in Flame's fur faded, they tingled slightly against her fingers and left a warm glow in her hands. "I'll look after you, don't worry . . . Oh, I just remembered, we're not allowed to have pets! Someone will notice if I keep you in my room. Felicity seems to have a thing about rules. She'll definitely tell someone."

Flame snuggled against her T-shirt. "I will use my magic so that only you may see and hear me."

"You can do that? Wow! That's

amazing, Flame!" Kara said. "Wait until I tell Cherry about you. I've got a feeling that she can keep a secret."

Flame reached up and touched her cheek with a tiny black-tipped paw. "You must tell no one, Kara. Promise me," he purred seriously.

Kara felt disappointed. This would have been such an exciting discovery to share with a new friend, but she nodded, determined to do whatever she must to keep Flame safe.

"All right. You'll be my secret," she said, cuddling his fluffy little body.

"Thank you, Kara," Flame purred contentedly.

"I'd better go down for lunch now, or the others will wonder where I am," Kara said. She put Flame down on the

rug and quickly put her sneakers on.
"Can you make yourself invisible now?"
she asked as they went out into the hall
together.

Flame nodded. "It is done."

He scampered at Kara's heels as she
went downstairs in search of the dining
room. Kara felt like pinching herself.
In her wildest dreams, she had never
imagined that she'd be sharing her time at
summer camp with a magic kitten!

"Over here!" Felicity called, pointing
at an empty seat as Kara and Flame
entered the busy dining room.

As Kara went over to her, two boys
barged past. One of them, a tough-looking
boy with short, spiky hair, deliberately
knocked against her arm.

"Hey! Watch out!" Kara cried, worried
that he was going to step on Flame.

"Watch out!" the boy copied, in a
silly baby voice. Laughing, he nudged his
friend, who wore glasses. The two of them
made faces at Kara before joining a group
of kids at a nearby table.

Kara glanced down worriedly. "Are
you okay, Flame?" she whispered.

"I am fine," Flame purred softly,
looking up at her.

Still feeling annoyed with the
rough boys, Kara sat between her new
roommates.

"Did that boy kick you?" Cherry
asked worriedly.

Kara shook her head. "No, but he
almost stepped on Fl—" She stopped,
realizing what she had been about to say.
"On my foot," she corrected herself
quickly. She was going to have to be a
lot more careful about keeping Flame a
secret!

"Those two are a pain. The big one's
called Nathan Potts, and the one with
glasses is Dan Weeks. They're in Magpies,"
Felicity said. "I saw them getting in
trouble for throwing crumpled-up potato-
chip bags at some pigeons."

"Charming," Kara said. Under the

table, she felt Flame jump up into her lap. As he settled down and started purring, she stroked his soft, fluffy fur.

The dining room was noisy with everyone chatting and laughing. The different groups of kids in Starlings, Magpies, Eagles, and Crows all sat at their own tables. Smaller tables with the adults, helpers, and organizers were dotted around the room.

Kara helped herself to a tuna sandwich. She checked that no one was watching and began passing tiny pieces under the table to Flame. He munched them hungrily, and as his rough little tongue licked her fingers, Kara smiled.

"Oh!" she suddenly gasped as she felt something hit her on the head.

A cookie dropped onto Kara's shoulder and then fell onto the floor. As she twisted around to see where it had come from, Flame sat up and rested his front paws on the table to look, too. Kara panicked briefly before remembering that only she could see Flame peering around the room. Another cookie hit her on the side of her face.

"Great shot, Nathan!" Dan Weeks cried.

"Who? Me?" Nathan rolled his eyes innocently as all the Magpies laughed.

"Those two are pathetic," Felicity said loudly.

Nathan's eyes narrowed. "Who are you calling pathetic?" He reached for two big bread rolls and drew back his arm, taking aim.

Kara began to feel a strange warm tingling feeling down her spine. She looked down to see big sparkles fizzing all over Flame's fur, and his whiskers crackling with electricity.

Kara caught her breath. Something strange was going to happen.

Chapter
THREE

Flame lifted one tiny black-
tipped paw and sent a stream of sparks
whooshing toward the Magpies'
table. As they sprinkled down onto
Nathan like a glittery shower, he sat
bolt upright and the rolls fell from his
fingers.

Kara watched in amazement as
Nathan reached out slowly and picked

up a half-empty bowl of pudding. He lifted the bowl up over his head and tipped it upside down. The pudding slopped out in a goopy mess, running down his face.

"Awesome!" Dan laughed and clapped his hands.

Nathan put down the empty bowl and sat there staring into space with a pyramid of pudding, topped by a cherry, decorating his head. Streamers of pudding dripped from his shoulders.

The whole dining room erupted with laughter. Felicity joined in and even Cherry was helpless.

While everyone was concentrating on Nathan, Kara glanced at Flame. "Oh, Flame. What have you done?" she scolded gently, looking into his mischievous green eyes.

"I am sorry, Kara. But I thought that boy might hurt you," Flame purred.

"Oh well, it serves him right for almost stepping on you," she whispered, stroking his tiny ears. The sparks in Flame's fur tickled briefly as they went out, and his glowing whiskers returned to normal.

Miss Cross stormed over to the Magpies' table. "What disgraceful behavior, Nathan Potts! That's no example to set the younger ones. And as for you, Daniel Weeks, I saw you egging him on!"

"Me? I didn't do anything!" Dan exclaimed, pushing his glasses more firmly onto his nose.

"Come with me, both of you!" Miss Cross ordered sternly. Dan stood up. But Nathan just sat there, looking confused. Dan nudged him. "Hey, Nathan, come on."

"What . . . ?" Nathan rose slowly to his feet. Sticking out his tongue, he licked a dribble of pudding off his cheek before following Dan and Miss Cross.

"All right, everyone. The fun's over now!" One of the adult helpers clapped his hands for silence. "Let's start cleaning up now, please. Here at Torc House, everyone pitches in."

Felicity looked horrified. "I didn't know we had to actually *work*! This is more like prison camp!"

Kara felt Flame jump down. She saw him scamper over to a windowsill, where he jumped up and then began to wash himself. She smiled to herself. It was going to be so fun having him around.

The next day after breakfast, Kara and Flame went to check the bulletin board where the day's activities were listed. Felicity and Cherry were already there. "Look, it says Starlings have hiking today, and then we have climbing, rappelling, and canoeing later in the week," Cherry said. "Sounds like fun!"

Felicity made a face. "Hiking sounds totally boring. I'm not doing it. I'll say I forgot to bring my sneakers or something."

Miss Cross was passing by. "Don't worry, Felicity, we have everything you'll need for all the activities. Hiking boots, spare socks, life jackets, you name it," she said helpfully. "But make sure you all remember your daily chores before you go."

Kara bit back a grin at the disgusted look on Felicity's face.

"Come on, Felicity. We're helping muck out the stables today," she said. "It'll be fun!"

Felicity didn't look convinced.

As they all entered the stable yard,

Kara saw Nathan and Dan. The boys
were being shown how to groom a
group of big gray ponies tethered outside
their stalls.

"Oh no, I just hope those two
behave themselves. They're worse when
they're together," she whispered to
Flame.

"I hope so, too," Flame mewed,
keeping a wary eye on them.

Some of the other Starlings and
Magpies were already at work. As Kara
passed the open door of the tack room,
she saw girls and boys inside polishing
saddles and cleaning harnesses. She and
Flame followed Cherry and Felicity into
the stables, where the familiar warm
smell of straw and ponies greeted them.

Kara thought of Amber at home in

her stable and felt a little sad. She hoped
her dad had remembered his promise to
give her pony extra cuddles. A soft nudge
at her ankle interrupted Kara's thoughts,
and she looked down to see Flame's tiny
face creased in concern.

"Is something wrong, Kara?" Flame
mewed softly.

"I'm okay. Thanks, Flame," Kara whispered back so that Cherry and Felicity wouldn't hear. She told him about the riding accident and Amber's strained leg.

Flame's bright green eyes twinkled with sympathy. "Will the animal doctor be able to make her better?"

"I don't know," Kara answered. "It's a really bad strain. Mom and Dad promised to let me know what the vet says." She sighed, making an effort not to worry.

A tall red-haired young man came over to the two of them, and Kara looked up expectantly. Flame's furry brow creased thoughtfully as he settled down by her feet.

"Hi, I'm Shane," the man said

to Kara and the girls with a friendly smile. "You'll find buckets, brooms, and a wheelbarrow over there. Have you mucked out before?"

"No," Felicity said, shuddering.

"I share a pony with my cousin. We look after her together," Cherry said shyly.

"*You* have a pony?" Felicity said, trying not to look impressed.

"I'm used to looking after my pony, too," Kara said.

"Great. I'll leave you to it, then. You girls can be in charge of showing your friend here what to do. I'll see you later," Shane said, walking away.

"Don't think you two are going to boss me around!" Felicity said. "Anyway, how hard can mucking out be? It's just stirring a bunch of dirty straw."

Kara pressed her lips together. Felicity was such a bossy know-it-all. "Here you go then, if you think you know what to do," she said, passing her a pitchfork.

Felicity tossed back her long hair and began jabbing half-heartedly at a pile of clean straw. Kara and Cherry left her to it. They got to work forking wet straw and droppings into a wheelbarrow.

"Ugh! It smells awful. How often do you have to do this?" Felicity complained loudly, wrinkling her nose, as the dirty straw began heaping up in the wheelbarrow.

"Every day. Sometimes twice in bad weather," Kara said.

"And I don't think it smells too bad. You get used to it," Cherry said.

"You must have something wrong

with your nose!" Felicity decided,
putting down her pitchfork and standing
with her hands in her pockets. As soon
as Kara and Cherry had filled the
wheelbarrow, she darted forward and
grabbed the handles. "I'll empty this,"
she said, wheeling it outside.

Kara and Cherry went and stood
in the doorway, watching as Felicity
wobbled her way across to the muck
heap. Flame scrabbled up the wooden
door and balanced on a beam near Kara.

As Felicity drew level to Nathan,
Kara saw the tough boy look up and
scowl at her. Felicity stuck her tongue
out at him. "I bet you got in *such* bad
trouble, didn't you?" she crowed. "You
looked like a total idiot with that
pudding all over you!"

"Shut up!" Nathan muttered.

But Felicity didn't stop. "I heard you lost a team point, too. I bet Magpies are pleased with you. Not!"

Kara saw Nathan's ears redden and his back stiffen. She felt a warning flicker. The tough boy was bad enough without Felicity making him worse.

"Just leave it, Felicity," she advised quietly.

"Huh! I was only sticking up for you!" Felicity said huffily, stomping past with her nose in the air.

Nathan went over to Dan, and the two of them stood close, talking.

"I wonder what those two are plotting now," Kara whispered to Flame.

Flame nodded, his eyes narrowing suspiciously.

Kara and Cherry went back into the stables. After sweeping, they spread clean straw in the stalls. Felicity wheeled the empty wheelbarrow back inside and then slouched against the door, examining her nails, as Kara and Cherry worked.

"Hey! Aren't you going to help?" Kara asked.

Felicity shrugged. "What's the point?

You two are doing fine by yourselves."

Kara didn't trust herself to answer. She finished making the ponies a clean bed as quickly as she could. "Phew! That's about it," she puffed, pushing back a strand of damp hair.

Shane came over just as they finished. "Good job, girls. Well done," he said nodding.

"Piece of cake!" Felicity chimed in, quickly standing up straight. "Come on, you two. I'm going to get ready for hiking."

Kara and Cherry looked at each other in disbelief. "She is *so* annoying," Cherry murmured.

Hiking might not be at the top of Kara's favorite-things-to-do list, but she had to admit that the views from the top of the windswept mountains were pretty amazing. Flame seemed to think so, too.

He had jumped out of her shoulder bag and sat looking at the flocks of sheep on the bright green slopes below them. They looked like tiny cotton balls.

"Wow! Look over there," Kara said, pointing to some circular, hump-shaped buildings with stone walls and ditches around them. "How old are they?"

Flame bounded up onto the roof of the nearest building and stood there with his head in the air. The wind ruffled his fluffy white fur as he snuffled the exciting smells.

"These must be about a million years old," Cherry said, peering into the low stone doorway. "Imagine living up here in the middle of nowhere!"

"You must be joking!" Felicity said with a shudder. "I bet there are huge hairy spiders in there!"

Kara nodded, agreeing with Felicity for once. "And it doesn't even have a TV!" she joked.

Cherry and Felicity laughed.

Kara could see Nathan and Dan messing around and laughing as they jumped off a low stone wall. She kept expecting them to come over, but when they ignored her and her friends, she began to relax. Kara sighed. *I'm probably worrying about nothing,* she told herself.

Chapter
FOUR

On the way back in the bus, one of the adult helpers started a sing-along, and everyone joined in. Nathan kept singing the wrong words and collapsing into giggles. Kara couldn't help laughing, too. Nathan was actually really funny when he wasn't being mean.

Back at Torc House, Kara and Cherry took cool drinks outside. Felicity went

upstairs to get Marvin before coming
back to join them on the lawn.

She sat down and cradled Marvin
in the crook of her arm. "Here we are!"
She put her soda can to the scruffy little
teddy bear's stitched mouth. "That's it,
slurp, slurp. Delicious," she crooned,
pretending to give Marvin a drink.

"That is *so* mushy," Cherry
commented.

Felicity ignored her.

Kara grinned as she turned onto
her stomach and sipped her lemonade.
Flame was stretched out beside her,
taking a nap. His tiny ears twitched and
his little black-tipped paws flexed as he
dreamed.

He looked so cute that Kara had to
concentrate on not reaching out and

stroking him, in case Cherry and Felicity wondered what she was doing.

"Who's making supper tonight? I'm starving," Cherry asked after a while.

"You can't be! The snacks you carry around would feed about two hundred people!" Felicity snorted.

"Oh ha, ha," Cherry said.

Kara hardly heard them. She was thinking about Amber again. She hoped that her sore leg wasn't hurting her too much.

As Flame stirred and sat up, yawning, Kara rose to her feet. "I think I'll call home and see if the vet's seen Amber yet," she decided.

Felicity jumped to her feet, too. "And I'm going to take Marvin back upstairs. He wants a nap now."

Cherry watched Felicity go, shaking
her head in disbelief, but smiling, too.
"It's kind of sweet that she's so fond of
that scruffy old teddy bear, isn't it?"

Kara nodded and smiled back.

✦

Kara's mom answered on the third
ring. "Hello, dear. I was just about to call
you. Are you having a good time?"

Kara said that she was, and excitedly

told her mom about sharing a room with Felicity and Cherry, and going hiking. She didn't think she should mention Flame, who was sitting invisibly at her ankles!

"Has the vet seen Amber, Mom?"

"Yes. He just left," Mrs. Parkes said. "There's not much to tell, I'm afraid. He still doesn't know if Amber's leg will heal properly. It's a matter of time."

Kara felt a lump rising in her throat. "But what if it never gets better? I might never be able to ride her again." She gulped.

"You can't think like that, dear. Let's just wait and see," her mom said gently. "Amber's young and healthy."

Kara's spirits were low as she said good-bye and hung up the phone. Flame wound himself around her ankles, rubbing against her sympathetically.

"I am sorry that you feel bad for Amber," he purred softly.

"Thanks, Flame," Kara said, reaching down to stroke him. She didn't feel like going to find Cherry and Felicity just yet. She wandered back up to the girls' dorm to be by herself for a while.

Flame scampered along alongside her.

As they got closer, Kara saw that the door to their room was wide-open. "That's weird," she said, puzzled.

Flame pricked up his ears. "There is someone inside."

Kara frowned as she moved closer until she also could hear muffled laughter.

"Quick! Someone's outside!" a familiar voice called out.

Two boys shot out. They ignored Kara and headed away without a backward glance. She heard their footsteps thudding down the stairs.

"Hey, stop! That was Nathan and Dan!" Kara cried. She rushed into the dorm. "Oh no!" she gasped.

All the pillows, comforters, and sheets had been dragged off the beds and piled up into a heap in the middle of the room. But that wasn't all. Her eyes widened in dismay as she realized that everything was soaking wet.

"I *knew* they were planning something. We'll never get all this stuff dry!" Kara said, clenching her fists.

"I've just about had enough of those two!"

Flame gave a little mew of sympathy. "Do not worry. I will help you."

Kara felt a familiar warm tingling up her spine. Flame's white fur ignited with silver sparkles, and his whiskers crackled with power.

She watched as Flame pointed a paw and sent a fountain of silver sparks toward the big pile of bedding. The sparks whipped into a sparkling tornado that spun faster and faster until it was just a glittering blur before Kara's eyes. The tornado zoomed all over the bedding, sucking up every last drop of water like a magic vacuum, before whizzing toward the nearby open window.

The spinning silver tornado flattened
as it squeezed through the window, and
once outside, the whole thing dissolved
in midair. Water poured down in a
torrent, just as if someone had tipped it
out of a huge bucket.

"Argh!" shrieked a voice from below.

"Help, I'm soaked," cried another
one.

Kara dashed to the window and stuck
her head outside.

Nathan and Dan stood there,
drenched to the skin. They must have
been waiting outside, gloating about their
mean trick—just in time to get caught in
the downpour.

A laugh bubbled up in Kara's throat.
"Oops! Bad luck!" she shouted.

Nathan glanced up. His face twisted.
"You threw that water on purpose. We'll
get you for that!" he yelled.

"I'd say we're even. Wouldn't you?"
Kara grinned as Nathan and Dan
squished away. She was still giggling
when she pulled her head back inside.
"That showed those two! Thanks again,
Flame!"

But Flame hadn't finished yet.
He pointed his little black paw at the
crumpled pile of bedding, and another

jet of silver sparks shot out.

Phwit! The whole pile of bedding
jumped into the air and shook out
their creases. *Rustle!* They divided into
three sets and marched in formation to
the beds like a line of soldiers. *Phloop!*
The sheet fitted itself onto the mattress,
the pillow plumped itself up, and the
comforter did a quick shimmy and settled
back into place.

Kara clapped her hands with delight.
Scooping Flame up, she kissed the top
of his fuzzy little head. "Wow! That was
amazing!" she said.

Flame purred and rubbed his face
against her arm affectionately. "I am glad
I could help."

She still was sitting on the bed
cuddling Flame when Felicity and

Cherry came in. Kara quickly sat up, thinking how strange it would look if she seemed to be holding an empty space.

Felicity marched straight up, a big grin on her face. "So it's true! It was you!"

Kara frowned. "What was me?"

"Nathan and Dan just came into the game room soaking wet," Cherry explained. "They said you leaned out the window and threw water all over them."

"Well, did you?" Felicity demanded.

"Yes, I did . . . ," Kara said and then she stopped. How was she going to explain what had happened? She couldn't tell them about the soaked beds, because then she'd have to explain how Flame had magically made them up again. "I did it because I . . . um, felt like it!"

"Good for you. I wish I'd seen their faces!" Cherry said, chuckling.

Suddenly, Felicity pointed at her bed and gave a loud shriek.

Kara and Cherry almost jumped out of their skins. "What?" they chorused.

"It's Marvin. He's gone!" Felicity said, horrified.

Kara looked over at her bed, where the old teddy bear was usually propped up against the pillow. It was true. Marvin was nowhere in sight. "Maybe he fell onto the floor. I'm sure he must be here somewhere."

"Kara's right. I'll help you look," Cherry said.

Between them they searched every corner of the room. Cherry even looked all the way under the bed, and Kara helped Felicity pull out the dressers so they could look in the narrow space behind them. But they didn't find Marvin.

Kara looked across at Flame, who was nosing around helpfully, trying to sniff out the teddy bear. An awful suspicion was dawning on her. "I think I know who took him," she whispered.

But Felicity had figured it out for herself. "Nathan and Dan stole him! And they won't give him back after what Kara just did to them. I'm never going to see

Marvin again!" She rounded on Kara, and her mouth twisted as she burst into noisy sobs. "It's all *your* fault! I hate you!"

Chapter
FIVE

Kara looked at Felicity in utter dismay. Why did she feel like a horrible criminal, when it wasn't even her fault?

She went over and put her arm around Felicity's shoulder. "Look, I'm really sorry about Marvin. Come on. Let's go and tell Miss Cross what happened."

"No, don't!" Felicity gulped.

"Nathan's not going to admit what he did. And if we tell on him, he . . . he could hurt Marvin."

"She's got a point," Cherry said. "It would be just like him to cut Marvin into tiny pieces and flush him down the toilet . . ." She faltered as Felicity gave an extra-loud wail. "Sorry."

"Okay," Kara said, thinking out loud. "Nathan's going to expect us to make a big deal about Marvin, isn't he? How about if we don't mention him and we pretend we don't care . . ."

"Don't care! Of all the heartless—" Felicity began.

"No, listen," Kara urged. "We only *pretend* we don't. Of course we're all very worried about poor Marvin, aren't we, Cherry?"

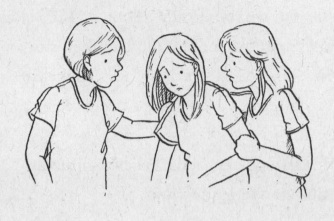

"Er . . . yeah," Cherry said.

"Okay, think about it, right? Nathan
won't be able to resist bragging about
stealing Marvin, will he? He'll probably
hold him ransom for a huge bar of
chocolate or something. And then we'll
have a chance of getting him back!" Kara
reasoned.

Felicity blinked tearfully. "Do you
think so?"

"Oh yes. No doubt about it," Kara said, sounding more confident than she felt. She dreaded to think how Felicity would react if Marvin was never seen again.

"Well, okay, then." Felicity sniffled. "But you better be right."

Over the next few days, Kara and Cherry made a huge effort to cheer up Felicity.

Felicity seemed to enjoy herself when Starlings went rappelling and then on a trip to a nearby carnival. But every night she just got into bed and pulled the comforter over her head, sniffling into her pillow.

"I don't know what to say to her," Kara whispered to Flame in the dark.

She knew that Felicity was lying there
awake, missing Marvin like crazy. Felicity
could be annoying, but she felt really sorry
for her. "Is there something you could do
to help her feel better?"

"Magic can fix lots of things, but it
cannot change people's feelings," Flame
mewed sadly.

The following morning, Kara and
Flame, Felicity and Cherry, and the other
Starlings were doing recycling as their
daily chore.

"The first week has gone by really quickly, hasn't it?" Cherry said, packing plastic bottles into a large container for collection.

Kara nodded, using a small handheld crusher to flatten soda cans into aluminum disks. Flame watched in fascination, skipping sideways and play growling as each can collapsed with a crackling sound. Kara smiled at his playful antics. Sometimes it was hard to remember that the cute kitten was a prince in his own world.

"I'm glad *you're* having fun," Felicity said moodily to Kara, catching her smiling to herself. She stamped hard on a small cardboard box to flatten it. "Your brilliant plan to pretend we don't care about Marvin was useless. Nathan has no

intention of ever giving him back. Have
you got any more fantastic ideas?"

Kara bit her lip, feeling awful. "Um . . .
not really."

"That's what I thought," Felicity
grumbled. "Thanks for nothing."

After chores were finished, Starlings
had wall climbing up the side of
Torc House. Wearing a safety harness
and helmet, Kara grasped the special

handholds to scale the wall and reach a wooden platform.

Flame bounded up beside her, jumping from place to place like a mountain goat. "This is very fun!" he mewed, giving Kara a whiskery grin.

Kara really enjoyed it, too, but the problem of Marvin was still on her mind.

"I don't get it," she said to Flame in the bathroom as she brushed her teeth that night. "Why haven't Nathan and Dan teased Felicity about stealing Marvin or asked her to buy him back or something?" She sighed deeply. "It's not their style to just keep him. Maybe we're wrong and they don't have him."

Flame's bright green eyes were thoughtful. "No. I think that you are right about those boys, Kara. I have a strong feeling that they are planning something."

"Well, we'll just have to wait and see, I guess," Kara said. "It's canoeing tomorrow. That should be good, and maybe it'll take Felicity's mind off Marvin."

Kara stood by the river with the other Starlings as she fastened the straps on her life jacket. The morning sun gleamed on the flowing water. Jeweled dragonflies flashed back and forth, hunting for flies.

She saw Felicity staring up the riverbank to where the Magpies were getting into canoes. Nathan and Dan were laughing and jostling each other as usual.

"Don't think about them. They're not worth it," Kara said.

"That's easy for you to say," Felicity said.

Kara sighed as she climbed into the large canoe beside Cherry. Flame jumped in after her, settling himself under Kara's seat and purring happily. Once the canoe was full, everyone picked up their oars and began to row.

Kara rowed in time with Cherry as the canoe floated smoothly downriver.

"This is great, isn't it?" Cherry said, pulling on her oar.

Everyone's oars splashed in time, and now and then a moorhen's call echoed across the water. Flame crawled out from under the seat. He stood up on his back paws and curled his front paw over the canoe's rim to peer curiously into the water.

"Be careful you don't fall in," Kara whispered.

The Magpies' canoe drew level with the Starlings' and then began to overtake them. Kara saw Nathan quickly lean over and put something into the water.

It was a small paper boat. Kara watched it floating toward her, bobbing up and down in the water. Propped up in it was a tiny familiar figure.

"Marvin! He's in that paper boat!" Felicity screeched. She let go of her oar and leaped to her feet.

As Felicity stumbled backward, the canoe rocked and then dipped low to one side. Kara leaned forward and grabbed at Flame, but her fingers closed on empty space. He gave a wail of alarm, and there was a tiny splash as Flame disappeared under the water.

Chapter
SIX

"Hey! Where did that kitten come
from?" Cherry cried, pointing at the water
as Flame's tiny head surfaced.

"Oh no!" Kara gasped. Everyone
could see Flame!

The shock of hitting the cold water
must have made him forget to be invisible.
Now he couldn't use his magic to save
himself without giving himself away!

Kara could see Flame's tiny legs moving frantically under the water. Would he be able to make it across the river? The opposite bank seemed a very long way away.

Suddenly she noticed that the Magpies' canoe was heading straight for Flame! They couldn't see him in the choppy water. "Look out for that kitten!" she screamed, her heart racing.

But the Magpies hadn't seen him, and their canoe was moving fast, closing in on Flame with every second. He would never be able to swim clear in time.

Kara didn't think twice. She leaped up out of her seat and jumped straight into the water. There was a huge splash and the cold took her breath away, but she bobbed up at once and her life jacket kept her afloat. Gasping, she kicked out strongly toward Flame and the canoe that was bearing down on him.

"Girl overboard!" Cherry shouted.

"There's the kitten!" someone shouted from the Magpies' canoe.

Kara recognized the voice. It was Nathan. She got a quick glance at his shocked white face as he pulled hard on one oar. The canoe swerved, just enough to miss Flame by a few inches. The wash from the Magpies' canoe swept Flame further away from Kara.

She kicked out harder as she saw that Flame's movements were getting weaker. The cold must be sapping his strength. Closer, closer. Almost there. She gave a final desperate lunge. Yes! She reached out and grabbed Flame by the scruff of his neck.

"Got you!" she cried. "You're safe now."

Flame coughed and spat out river water. Scrabbling up her life jacket, he clung to her shoulder, shivering and whimpering.

As Kara struck out toward the bank with Flame, all the kids in the canoes started cheering and waving. She swam one-handed and waved back to show she was all right.

A soggy object, already half under water, drifted near her hand.

The paper boat with Marvin inside!

On impulse, Kara scooped it up and stuffed it into the top of her life jacket. A few minutes later she reached shallow water. She waded through the muddy reeds and climbed out of the river. Finally she flopped down to catch her breath.

Flame jumped down onto the grass beside her. He looked even smaller than usual, with his wet fur plastered to his tiny body. He placed a tiny, black-tipped paw on her arm and blinked up at her with bright emerald eyes. "Thank you for saving me. You were very brave, Kara," he purred.

She smiled down at him fondly. "I wasn't really. I just couldn't bear to see you in danger." It was true, she realized. She hated to think of anything happening to her friend.

"Kara! Are you all right?" Miss Cross called, steering the Starlings' canoe into the bank. Felicity, Cherry, and the other Starlings all jumped onto the grass and helped drag the canoe out of the water.

"Quick! You better hide until they're gone. Otherwise they'll make a big deal about it and try to find out who you belong to!" Kara whispered to Flame.

Flame nodded. With a swish of his tail, he darted into the nearby reeds.

Miss Cross stormed up the bank with Felicity and Cherry close behind her.

"Uh-oh! Now I'm in for it," Kara breathed.

"What possessed you to jump in, you silly girl?" Miss Cross scolded. "It was a very dangerous thing to do! You almost capsized the canoe and had us all in the water!"

"Er . . . um . . . ," Kara stammered, playing for time. She leaned forward as she rose to her feet, and the soggy paper boat and teddy bear tipped out of her life jacket and fell onto the grass.

"Marvin!" Felicity shrieked, swooping down to grab her teddy bear. "I thought he was gone forever." She turned shining eyes on Kara. "Thank you so much for saving him! I'll never forget this," she said, and then her face became serious. "Leave this to me," she whispered, turning to Miss Cross. "It was my fault, Miss," she said in a louder voice. "When I saw Nathan put poor Marvin in that paper boat, I was so shocked that I stood up. That's when the canoe almost overturned and Kara fell out."

"Fell out? But I saw Kara jump in . . . ," Miss Cross said, looking puzzled.

Felicity widened her blue eyes innocently. "Oh no, Miss. It might have looked like that, but she definitely fell in. You can ask Cherry. She was nearest to Kara."

"Felicity's right, Miss. I saw everything," Cherry said firmly.

"Well, maybe I was mistaken. It all happened so fast. What about that kitten?

Did anyone see what happened to it?"
Miss Cross asked.

"I . . . er, think it ran off. It . . . was
probably . . . a stray. *Brrr-rrr-rr.*" Kara's teeth
started to chatter. She hugged herself to
try to stop shivering.

"Oh dear. You should get out of those
wet clothes before you catch a cold," Miss
Cross said, looking concerned. "I'll drive
you back to Torc House. The rest of you,
wait here for me, please. I'll be back as
soon as I can."

As Kara climbed into the bus and sat
down, Flame jumped onto the seat next to
her, purring loudly.

Twenty minutes later, Kara was drying
herself after a long hot shower. Flame sat
on the bath mat, waiting for her.

Kara pulled on a bathrobe. "That's better. I feel like a new person." Picking Flame up, she cuddled him and then wrinkled her nose. "Phew! Muddy river water! How would you like a bath in the sink?"

"No, thank you. I have already been wet today!" Flame mewed indignantly.

"Yes, and excuse me for saying so, but

you stink!" Kara said. "Come on. It won't take long, and then I'll dry you with the hair dryer. You'll like that."

Flame looked down his tiny nose doubtfully. "I am not sure that I will. But, very well, I trust your word."

Kara bathed him gently, taking great care to keep shower gel far away from his eyes and ears. She rinsed him in warm water and then patted him dry with a towel. "Let's go into the bedroom. There's no one in there."

Flame sat on Kara's lap as she switched the hair dryer on to a low setting. At first he tensed at the unfamiliar noise and laid his ears back, but he gradually relaxed as the warm air ruffled his fur.

"Nice?" Kara asked.

Flame gave a hesitant purr. "It feels very strange, but I like it very much."

Kara smiled, wondering if anyone else had ever bathed a lion prince! "There," she said a few minutes later as she put the hair dryer away. "Now you're all dry and you smell wonderful." *And you look like a fuzzy ball of cotton,* she thought, swallowing a giggle in case she hurt his pride.

Flame jumped onto her bed and kneaded the comforter into a soft nest. Kara curled herself around him. She only intended to relax for a few minutes, but it was almost two hours later when Felicity and Cherry came bursting in.

"Guess what! Nathan and Dan have lost more team points *and* they've been grounded," Cherry said.

Kara sat up rubbing her eyes. "Really?" she said, quickly shifting so that she sat in front of the tiny dent Flame made.

"Yeah, they have to stay inside Torc House tomorrow and miss out on the barbecue," Felicity said gleefully. "I think they should have been grounded for about ten years after what they did to Marvin!" She held up the tattered teddy bear, which looked even more bedraggled than usual after his soaking.

Kara smiled as Felicity exaggerated as usual. But at least Felicity was happy again, and they might all get a good night's sleep.

Chapter
SEVEN

"Why is it that time passes so quickly when you're having a good time?" Kara said to Flame as she changed out of her sports clothes a few days later.

Flame shook his head. "I do not know, but I have noticed this, too," he purred.

Kara had just finished a tennis match. Starlings had been playing against

Magpies, and Magpies had won by two sets to one.

Cherry and Felicity came into the locker room. "Nathan's a great player. I really enjoyed the match," Cherry commented, wiping her forehead with the back of her hand. "He's actually really funny when he's not being mean."

Kara nodded. She had noticed that, too. Nathan and Dan had been on their best behavior for days now. Maybe they had really learned their lesson this time. And Kara remembered it was Nathan calling out that had made the Magpies turn their canoe in time to miss hitting Flame.

"Only two days left now. I thought I'd really miss home, but now I wish

I was going to be here for a month," Felicity said glumly.

"At least there's the group pony ride to look forward to. I can't wait," Cherry said.

"Me too. I haven't been riding since Amber hurt her leg," Kara said. She had spoken to her parents the night before, but there was no more news about Amber.

"I'm sorry about Amber," Felicity said unexpectedly. She came over and put an arm around Kara's and Cherry's shoulders. "I know I can be a pain, but you've both been really nice to me. Can we promise to keep in touch when we get home?" she asked.

Kara was touched. She looked over at Cherry. Cherry blushed, looking really happy.

"Deal!" they chorused.

The following day, Kara peered out of the dorm window at the sunlit mountains. The slopes looked fresh and bright, and the peaks showed grayish purple against the blue sky.

"Look, Flame. It's a purr-fect day for pony riding!" she joked.

Flame didn't answer, but he gave a
muffled little meow.

Kara turned back to her bed in
surprise. Usually he was up and about by
now, his tiny face alight with anticipation,
but today he was still buried deep beneath
the comforter.

"Come on, sleepyhead. Time to go,"
she urged, digging a hand under the

comforter and tickling him gently. "I need to go and get into my riding gear. Cherry and Felicity have already gone."

Flame poked his head out, revealing dull fur and flattened ears. His whiskers quivered as his whole body trembled. "I cannot come with you, Kara."

Kara froze, her teasing smile fading. "What's wrong? Do you not feel well?"

Flame shook his head. "I sense my enemies drawing near."

"Oh no!" Alarm shot through Kara's body. She had almost convinced herself that this day would never come. Now it was here. And Flame was in terrible danger. "What can I do to help you? Should I stay here with you?"

"No. It is better if you go riding with the others. So many ponies

moving around on the mountain may
confuse my uncle's spies."

Kara nodded slowly. What Flame
said made sense, but she hated to leave
him. He seemed so tiny and vulnerable.
"But I might never see you again
or . . . or get the chance to say good-
bye," she said hesitantly.

"I will find you later, if I can,"
Flame promised, looking up at her
with troubled emerald eyes, before
turning and crawling back under the
comforter.

Kara desperately wanted to pick
him up and cuddle him better, but
she knew she had to be very brave
and leave him there as he had asked.
She took a deep breath and went out
quickly. "Good luck, Flame," she said

in a small, trembling voice. "Please take care and I really, really hope I'll see you later."

The stable yard was swarming with Starlings, Eagles, Crows, Magpies, and adult helpers as everyone mounted their ponies.

Kara swung her leg over Shamrock, and sat down in the saddle. She was trying hard not to think about Flame and to look forward to the day's riding.

"Are you all right?" Cherry asked from her pony, Flossie.

Felicity's pony was called Daisy. She looked over and smiled at Kara. "I just know Amber's going to be fine," she said.

"Thanks," Kara said, wishing she

could tell her friends that she was more worried about Flame right now. As she imagined the fierce cats combing the mountain slopes for a scent of their tiny royal prey, a shiver ran down her back.

"Lead the way, Starlings!" called Miss Cross from her bay horse.

Cherry, Felicity, and Kara moved their ponies forward, and the long line of ponies made their way up the mountain path.

As they rose higher, Kara could see the blue lakes and colorful woodland of the national park spreading out far below her. Shamrock was a beautiful, gentle pony and moved very smoothly up the steep path. Kara wished she could enjoy it all much more than she was able to right now.

When everyone dismounted for a picnic, Kara sat with Cherry, Felicity, and the other Starlings. Everyone else seemed to be chatting and enjoying the warm sunshine. But as Kara remounted Shamrock, she noticed that clouds were gathering.

They had barely begun the return journey when a mist began to descend. Within minutes, the mountaintops were blanked out.

"Keep close together, everyone," Miss Cross called from up front. "We don't want anyone to become separated."

At least Flame's enemies should have a hard time finding him, too, Kara thought hopefully. She peered ahead as Shamrock picked her way steadily down the track. "That's it, girl. Steady now."

"I don't like this. It's a little spooky, isn't it?" Felicity said beside her.

Kara nodded. It was amazing how different everything looked. On the way up, the mountains were bright and friendly. Now the trees made mysterious shapes, and the ponies and riders ahead of them were smudges of shadow.

"The mist's still getting thicker. I can hardly see four yards in front of me now," Kara said worriedly. Suddenly a cry and a snort of alarm came from behind her. She halted Shamrock and turned in the saddle. "What's wrong?"

"It's Flossie! She's refusing to move. I can't get her to budge," Cherry called worriedly.

Kara carefully turned Shamrock and rode up to Cherry. "Give me Flossie's reins. I'll try leading her," she suggested.

"Good idea," Cherry said.

Kara held Flossie's reins and urged Shamrock forward slowly, but Flossie whinnied and dug in her heels. "It's no good. I think she's spooked by the mist."

"Hey! What's the holdup? You're blocking the way!" Nathan called, halting beside Kara and Cherry. Dan was close behind him.

"It's Flossie. She won't move. Maybe she cast a shoe or something," Kara explained.

"No problem. We'll ride down and tell Miss Cross and the others. There's a shortcut down here. I saw it on the way up. Come on, Dan!" Nathan said.

"No, don't go off the path!" Kara said in alarm. "You'll get lost."

Nathan squared his shoulders. "No way! I know what I'm doing."

As Nathan and Dan steered their ponies down the slope, Flossie gave a sudden lurch forward after them and pulled her reins out of Kara's hands. Cherry wobbled, almost losing her balance, and then leaned forward and wrapped her arms around Flossie's neck.

"Cherry!" Felicity cried. "Come on, Daisy, after her!"

Kara had no choice. She squeezed Shamrock on and followed the others, hoping desperately that Nathan knew where he was going. The thick mist had muffled all sound, and it left fine droplets on the ponies' manes.

Suddenly, pony shapes seemed to loom up at Kara. "Oh," she gasped, just managing to stop before she rode into Nathan, Dan, Cherry, and Felicity. "What's wrong? Why did you all stop?"

"Because we're lost, that's why!" Felicity said. "Admit it, Nathan. Your stupid idea about taking a shortcut was useless!"

"Okay. But I was just trying to help! It wasn't *my* pony that totally panicked, was it?" Nathan snapped back.

"It's no use arguing," Kara said quickly before they could start fighting. "We have to decide what to do."

"Kara's right. We can't see a thing in this mist. There could be a steep drop just feet away," Cherry said.

"Don't be silly," Nathan said, but Kara thought he sounded worried.

"Look, once the mist clears, we'll be able to see where we are," Kara reasoned, sounding calmer than she felt.

"But what if it doesn't?" Felicity gulped. "I'm already cold and I don't want to stay up here all night."

Me neither, Kara thought.

She shivered and fought a sudden wave of panic. If only Flame were here. He'd be able to help. But Flame had to fight his own battle, hiding from his uncle. It looked like they were by themselves.

Chapter
EIGHT

Kara stood beside a large rock, holding
Shamrock's reins. Cherry, Felicity, Dan,
and Nathan also had dismounted. They
stood close together in silence, thinking
about what they should do.

The clammy mist swirled around
them, and now the light was fading.
"Easy, girl," Kara said reassuringly, stroking
Shamrock's cheek as the pony shifted

nervously. She wasn't looking forward
to a cold, dark, scary night on the
mountain.

Suddenly, out of nowhere, a tiny
glowing shape appeared on top of the
rock. Kara felt a furry head rubbing
against her cold hand, and then a rough
little tongue licked her fingers.

"Flame!" she whispered delightedly. "You're safe! I didn't think I'd ever see you again."

"I told you I would find you if I could. My enemies have passed by. But if they come back, I will have to leave at once," he mewed softly.

Kara beamed at him. "I'm just so glad you're here now!" she whispered. "We're lost, and it's cold and almost dark. There's no way we can risk getting down."

Flame's eyes brightened thoughtfully. "I will be back soon," he purred, leaping into the mist and disappearing. He was back almost at once. "I have found somewhere for you all to shelter. Follow me," he urged, beckoning with a fluffy front paw.

Kara looked across at the others.
"Okay, everyone. I, uh . . . just
remembered seeing a map of the
mountain back at Torc House. If we
go this way, we'll find shelter," she said,
pointing to where Flame was glowing
softly in the mist.

Nathan looked suspicious. "What
map? I didn't see one."

"Who cares? If no one has a better
idea, I'm going after Kara," Felicity said.

"So am I," Cherry said.

"Me too. Come on, Nathan. It's totally
creepy here," Dan urged.

Kara led the small procession after
Flame, keeping her eyes on his tiny
sparkling form as he scampered up the
steep slope. Barely five minutes passed
before a dark shape loomed out of the

mist, and Shamrock almost stumbled
through a gap in a low stone wall.

"It's okay, everyone. Here it is!" Kara
called over her shoulder.

Kara realized that they had found
the old stone buildings from where
they'd been hiking the other day. She
saw Flame run inside the smallest of
them. As Kara tethered Shamrock, a
familiar warm prickling tickled her
spine. While the others were seeing to
their ponies, she quickly followed Flame
inside.

She saw sparks ignite in Flame's fur,
and his whiskers fizzled with power. He
lifted a tiny paw and sent a whoosh of
sparks zooming around the stone hut.

Snap! A rusty old lamp on a hook
lit up by itself. *Crackle!* A small fire

appeared in the fireplace. *Rustle* and *thud!*
Firewood piled itself up neatly, and a layer
of clean, dry bracken spread itself across
the floor.

The very last sparks had just faded
from Flame's coat when Felicity came in.
"Wow! It's really cozy in here," she said,
looking impressed. "How did you light the
fire and stuff, Kara?"

"Mom taught me survival skills. She
used to be in Girl Scouts," Kara fibbed.

Nathan, Dan, and Cherry also looked
around in amazement as they came in.
Cherry investigated a dusty stone shelf.
"Look, tin cups and a pot of water. It
smells fresh. It should be okay if we boil
it."

"Boiled water, delicious," Nathan said,
making a face.

Cherry grinned and dug into her backpack. "How about hot chocolate, potato chips, and cookies?"

Nathan cheered, and Kara joined in with a grin.

Felicity gave Cherry a hug. "You're a star! I'll never tease you about carrying snacks around again!" she promised.

Dan suddenly remembered his cell phone. He called Torc House to tell everyone they were safe, before settling down. "They know where we are.

Someone's coming to get us as soon as the mist clears," he told them.

An hour later, after they'd eaten, everyone curled up on the dry bracken. Cherry, Felicity, Nathan, and Dan fell asleep right away, but Kara lay awake, cuddling Flame.

"Thanks again for coming to find me. You're the best friend ever," she whispered sleepily.

"You are welcome, Kara," Flame purred, and snuggled against her.

Kara fell asleep with her cheek against Flame's soft fur. When she woke, the lantern was low, and it was dark inside the little hut. As she stirred, she felt Flame stiffen and then leap out of her arms. She opened her eyes just in time to see him bounding out the door.

"Flame?"

With suspicion rising up in her, she got up and quietly went outside after him. Suddenly, from the pitch-black night came a blinding silver flash. The tethered ponies twitched their ears, but none of them made a sound.

Kara blinked hard as her sight cleared. Flame stood there as his magnificent real self. Sparks gleamed in the majestic young white lion's dazzling coat, and his emerald eyes glowed. An older gray lion with a wise face stood next to Flame.

And then Kara knew that this time Flame was leaving for good.

"Your enemies are very close. We must go," the gray lion rumbled.

Flame raised a huge white paw in

farewell. "Be well, Kara," he said in a
deep velvety purr.

Kara's throat closed with tears, and
there was an ache in her chest. "Good-
bye, Flame," she whispered hoarsely.
"Take care."

There was a final bright flash, and
Flame and the older lion disappeared.

Kara glimpsed the sinister outline of his uncle's spies against the dark night and heard a shriek of rage before they, too, disappeared.

There was a sound behind her, and Cherry, Felicity, Nathan, and Dan came tumbling outside. "What's happening?" Felicity murmured sleepily. "Are you okay? We heard voices."

"Kara? Felicity?" Miss Cross's head appeared above the low stone wall, and the beam of a flashlight swung toward them. "And Nathan and Dan, too. Here they all are, safe and sound!" she called to someone over her shoulder, and then she turned back with a frown. "I think someone has some serious explaining to do! But first," she said with a twinkle in her eye, "I have a message for you, Kara.

Your parents called just before we left.
They said to tell you that the vet says
Amber's leg is almost better. It's healed like
magic."

"Really?" Kara gasped.

Somehow she knew that this was
Flame's final gift to her. A dart of pure joy
seemed to pierce her sadness. "Thank you
so much, Flame. I'll never forget you," she
whispered.

She couldn't wait to go home to take care of Amber and tell her all about her exciting adventures with her magical friend!

About the Author

Sue Bentley's books for children often include animals or fairies. She lives in Northampton, England, and enjoys reading, going to the movies, and sitting watching the frogs and newts in her garden pond. If she hadn't been a writer, she would probably have been a skydiver or brain surgeon. The main reason she writes is that she can drink pots and pots of tea while she's typing. She has met and owned many cats, and each one has brought a special sort of magic to her life.

Don't miss these Magic Kitten books!

#1 A Summer Spell

#2 Classroom Chaos

#3 Star Dreams

#4 Double Trouble

#5 Moonlight Mischief

#6 A Circus Wish

#7 Sparkling Steps

#8 A Glittering Gallop

#9 Seaside Mystery

#11 A Shimmering Splash

A Christmas Surprise

Purrfect Sticker
and Activity Book

Starry Sticker
and Activity Book

Don't miss these Magic Ponies books!

Don't miss these Magic Puppy books!

Don't miss these Magic Bunny books!

#1 Chocolate Wishes

#2 Vacation Dreams

#3 A Splash of Magic

#4 Classroom Capers

#5 Dancing Days